The
Cried *Help*

by Leslie Barbosa
illustrated by *Lane Yerkes*

Copyright © by Harcourt, Inc.

All rights reserved. No part of this publication may be reproduced or transmitted in any form or by any means, electronic or mechanical, including photocopy, recording, or any information storage and retrieval system, without permission in writing from the publisher.

Requests for permission to make copies of any part of the work should be mailed to the following address: School Permissions, Harcourt, Inc., 6277 Sea Harbor Drive, Orlando, Florida 32887-6777.

HARCOURT and the Harcourt Logo are trademarks of Harcourt, Inc.

Printed in the United States of America

ISBN 0-15-317311-4 – The Pig Who Cried Help

Ordering Options
ISBN 0-15-318656-9 (Package of 5)
ISBN 0-15-316987-7 (Grade 3 Package)

2 3 4 5 6 7 8 9 10 179 02 01 00

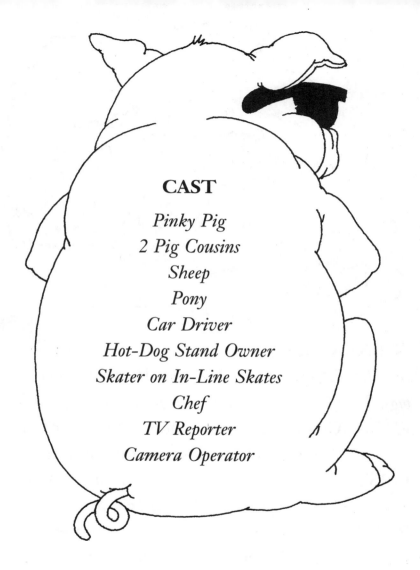

CAST

Pinky Pig
2 Pig Cousins
Sheep
Pony
Car Driver
Hot-Dog Stand Owner
Skater on In-Line Skates
Chef
TV Reporter
Camera Operator

SCENE ONE

(PINKY PIG is carrying a suitcase. We see two other pigs. They have their snouts in their food, eating noisily.)

PINKY: Cousins, get your snouts out of your food and listen to me. It's time for me to leave.

FIRST COUSIN *(looking up from the food)*: Where are you going? *(She goes back to eating.)*

PINKY: To the city. Don't all try to stop me at once.*(The pigs ignore him and keep on eating. A few tumbleweeds drift by.)*

PINKY: You know, many farm animals have made
their fortunes in the big city.
SECOND COUSIN: Is that so? What pig needs a
fortune? *(grunts, then goes back to eating)*
PINKY: I give up. *(He picks up his bag, steps over
some tumbleweeds, and walks offstage.)*

SCENE TWO

(A city street. PINKY is looking around, scared.)

PINKY *(to himself)*: This place is large. And scary. And loud. Instead of tumbleweeds, there are bikes. Instead of cows, cars. At least I have friends here. My friends Sheep and Pony both said to look them up when I got to the city. *(PONY and SHEEP walk onstage.)*

PINKY: My friends! I've found you! Have you made your fortunes yet?

SHEEP: Uh, no. I still have hope, though. I've got this idea for an alarm clock. Sounds just like a sheep. It goes 'Baaa, Baaa.'

PONY: That will never work. You've got to get a
job to make your fortune. I have a job
giving rides at the children's zoo. What's
your plan, Pinky?

PINKY *(puts on sunglasses)*: I plan to be a movie
star.

SHEEP: BAAH!

PONY: HA! *(They laugh and slap their knees.)*

PINKY *(to audience)*: Yes, I will! I just know it!

SCENE THREE

(PINKY is walking on the street. A car with DRIVER zooms by. The horn is blaring loudly.)

PINKY: Oh, help! HELP! WHERE ARE MY FRIENDS?

SHEEP *(runs onstage, out of breath)*: What's wrong?

PINKY *(with great drama)*: I'm in danger!

SHEEP: What danger? Where? **There?** That's a car horn!

PINKY *(unembarrassed)*: Oh. Well, it **could** have been trouble.

6

SCENE FOUR

(The next day. PINKY is on his way to an audition for a play.)

PINKY: Help! A huge silver thing is coming right for me! I'M IN DANGER! GET OVER HERE!

PONY *(looks around, unworried)*: What's wrong, Pinky?

PINKY *(upset)*: That—that silver thing was heading right for me! I was so scared I couldn't even budge!

PONY: That's a hot-dog cart! When you see one rolling your way, you'd **better** budge, or you could end up with a broken snout. *(muttering to himself)* For this, I left the zoo.

7

(PONY trots offstage, shaking his head.)

PINKY: Oh. Well, it **could** have been trouble.
Oh, no! What's that? More wheels!
Help! HELP!

SHEEP *(running, out of breath)*: Pinky, Pinky,
Pinky. That's only a skater. Those wheels
on his feet are skates. Don't call me again.
Do you understand?

PINKY *(nods and sniffs)*: I understand. I shall not
bother you again.

8

SCENE FIVE

(A man dressed as a CHEF comes onstage. He goes to a phone booth and picks up the phone.)

PINKY *(to himself)*: I shall not call for help again. Uh, oh. Who is that suspicious-looking man talking on the phone? I will make myself invisible and find out. *(PINKY hides and listens to the phone call.)*

CHEF: Yes, boss. I won't come back to the restaurant until I have found a pig. Right. The fresher, the better.

PINKY *(draws back in horror)*: Oh, now I wish I were really invisible.

CHEF *(sees PINKY)*: Hey!

PINKY *(as loudly as he can)*: HELP! *(PINKY dashes away.)*

SCENE SIX

(PINKY has run into the park. There are trees and grass.)

PINKY: I have to think fast. Hey, I have an idea! *(PINKY poses on one leg as if he were a statue. The CHEF dashes in with a suspicious look on his face. He runs past PINKY.)*

PINKY: He ran right by me! I'm safe!

(TV REPORTER and CAMERA OPERATOR hurry into the park, as PINKY still poses.)

REPORTER *(to CAMERA OPERATOR)*: There!
Get me some pictures of this pig! *(He
turns to PINKY, who is still posing.)* Hey,
pig! What are you doing?

PINKY *(with great feeling)*: Saving myself!

REPORTER: What do you mean?

PINKY: A bad man wants to make me into bacon.
*(The CAMERA OPERATOR begins taking
pictures. PINKY smiles a movie-star smile.)*
How did you find me?

REPORTER: This park is right near a TV
station. I was looking out of the window.
I saw the whole thing!

11

SCENE SEVEN

(PINKY, dressed as a TV star with scarf and sunglasses, is being interviewed by the TV REPORTER. SHEEP and PONY are nearby, looking upset.)

REPORTER: So that's the story of how Pinky Pig got his big break in show business. This reporter was proud to meet such a wonderful star. How does it feel to be the world's most famous pig?

PINKY: Great, just great. And I want to say that I never forget my friends. Thank you, Pony and Sheep, for not saving me. You did me a favor.

SHEEP *(to PONY)*: Baah. Next time, let's just save him. *(PONY nods.)*

Add a Scene

On a sheet of paper, write one additional scene for the play. Include some of the characters you've already met. Be sure to write the stage directions.

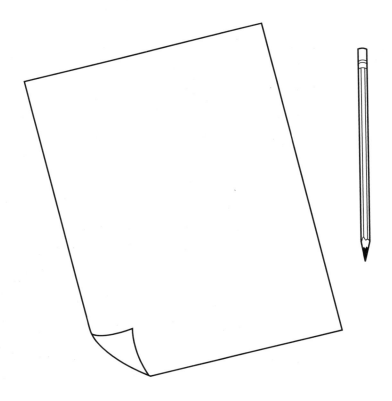

School-Home Connection You may wish to divide up the characters and read this play aloud with your child. Your child might also like to make stick puppets for the characters and perform the play as a puppet show.